Brighten the Corner Stories Too:

Affirmations For Children of Color

by Nurseen Legair Davis

Brighten the Corner Stories Too: Affirmations For Children of Color

Copyright© Nurseen Legair Davis

ISBN   978-1-7367669-0-3

Publication date February 27, 2021

To order additional copies of this book, contact: Nurseen Legair Davis at nurseendavis@gmail.com

Dedication

This book is dedicated to my grandchildren: Jalen Rogers, Kyleigh Rogers, Wellington Rogers, Zurie Augustin, Zahir Augustin, and Zayan Augustin who continue to inspire me to write, to children who are struggling to accept their circumstances, and those who are seeking a better life and a better experience.

Acknowledgments

Special thanks to my grandchildren who have continued to be my motivation to write so they can be inspired to be the best version of themselves. Thanks to Erma Skelton, Pearlette Mitchell, Meloney Dawes, and Joan Legair, for their editing skills. Special thanks to my daughter, Cozette, who inspired me to construct these affirmations. Thanks to my husband, Charles Davis, my dear friend, Dr. Martha Joseph Watts, and all my family members for their continuous support and encouragement. Most of all, I thank my Creator for implanting the ideas in my head and providing me with the skills to compose the entries.

TABLE OF CONTENTS

1

Loving Me, In and Out

So many children, especially girls, are struggling with loving themselves because of the pressure they encounter. They wish they looked like another person. They wish for others' hair, complexion, and other physical attributes. Then, the pressures from social media cause them to extend themselves to look and sound like popular personalities. The idea that beauty is found within is not always understood. As a result, many children spend their time seeking to alter their physical attributes.

There once was a girl with a very beautiful face,

but was told she was ugly and began to work in haste

to change her appearance; I wished she were not fazed.

She looked in the mirror with tears in her eyes

because she inspected herself in a critical light.

For months, she stared in the mirror and tossed back and forth,

confused as to what she wanted to tackle first.

Not satisfied with what people could see,

she whispered, "I want to make over a better me."

Ignoring true qualities that make her on the inside,

believing that her beauty was solely on the outside.

She looked at her face, at every angle,

preparing a remedy, ready to tangle.

The kinky hair texture was abruptly rejected.

She permed it to mimic what was more accepted.

Was given a wig, though blonde, was not rejected.

Her dark chocolate skin, they constantly teased.

She was ready to alter and apply bleaching cream.

The nose, she was told, was somewhat flared.

So, she pondered procedures to have it repaired.

Her dark brown eyes she thought were not so pleasing.

Colored contacts, she said, looked much more appealing.

Eyelashes, eyeshadows, bold lips, and contouring,

created a new person. The face was stunning!

She complained she was fat; in her mind, that's what the mirror
    said.

So, she forsook diet and exercise and became bulimic instead.

And when it began to threaten her health,

the consequences were what she was dealt.

She sought help and was strongly admonished

to love herself and that habit she must abolish.

The efforts to look more beautiful were causing much pain.

All the make-up and makeovers were driving her insane.

Then one day, as she washed all the make-up off her face,

she took a good look at herself in the mirror and was amazed.

The sparkle in her eyes now she saw.

A smile so radiant flashed back at her.

That moment she regretted all the things she did

to make herself over into that new person she rebuilt.

It hit her, that beauty she sought, is a temporary thing.

Her humility and good character are what true beauty brings.

Nothing is wrong with the outward adorning.

But a true love of self requires an inside cleansing.

Unselfishness, kindness, and love, she agrees, are combinations

that will show her true beauty and will allow her to accept her

imperfections.

A fool she thought she was, to believe in the "beauty laws."

And so, she no longer wears a mask to cover her flaws.

She now is aware that beauty lies more within.

It's a permanent thing, much deeper than her skin.

2

The New School Challenge

Teenagers today are faced with many obstacles. Some have ways of freeing themselves, while others have difficulty coping. Sometimes it may be the challenge of entering a new school or perhaps dealing with a lack of acceptance by peers. It takes a lot of encouragement and a strong will to weave through the daily challenges to persevere and triumph through it all.

This story isn't new. It has oftentimes been repeated.

The girl moved to a new school and has been mistreated.

Gladly, her story didn't end the same as others.

She pushed back and took back all her powers.

She attended a school close to her new neighborhood.

The family moved to escape the troubles in the hood.

At first it was a big struggle.

This black girl was in a bubble.

Afraid of the students and how they would receive her,

she stayed by herself and just observed their behaviors.

The first week of school she was somewhat perplexed.

They ignored her and stared; the atmosphere complex.

She sat all alone that day in the cafeteria.

Then a brunet girl came to give her the criteria:

"It will be hard for you to make friends here.

You are different, maybe won't be treated so fair.

Just listen to us and take part in what we do.

And if you're lucky, we can definitely reward you."

She shrugged, having no intention

to conform to the girl's suggestions.

The teacher did little to make her more comfortable.

Teacher said no need to; everyone is approachable.

She wanted the opportunity to sit with new friends and talk.

She longed for the time she and a friend can take a walk.

Every time she made an attempt,

she was met with a lot of contempt.

Many who looked like her were on the football team,

but not even a glimpse at her direction she gleaned.

Oh, what an uncomfortable feeling!

She felt so odd and not belonging.

But she stood firm as she was put to the test.

And she discovered it was all for the best.

She made up her mind that she had what it took

to go the distance by simply beating the books.

She did every assignment with no objection,

and she made no mistakes, pure perfection.

She pulled out her books and used the skills she acquired.

And read everything in sight, even though it was not required.

Much knowledge she gained just from the extra reading.

And took part in quiz bowl, and science bowl and spelling.

And she advanced in every school competition.

Now, the other students looked at her to get some inspiration.

She took her negative experience and turned it into motivation.

She advanced herself, and in all areas performed with excellence,

and proved she can succeed when she used her intelligence.

Now she feels very accomplished.

Her skills are intact and polished.

In the face of hardship and wrongs,

she remained steadfast and strong.

And became a good example and success story,

of overcoming obstacles by not sitting down and worry.

3

The Unseen Dad and Super Mom

Kia has two beautiful friends with whom she visits periodically. They both live with their mother and father. Kia enjoys visiting with them because she likes to communicate and play games with their dads and other family members. Kia has never met her dad and frequently feels the void of his absence. Sometimes she feels odd that he's not around, but she takes comfort knowing that her friends share their dads with her, and her mama provides all her needs:

It was a recurring dream that I had.

In my dream I saw my lost Dad.

And although my mom is forever present,

it was a joy to acknowledge my father's presence.

Dad, in my dream, is as strong as a tower.

When I'm lost and afraid, he gives me power.

I see him as a powerful king.

In my eyes he can do anything.

Big and strong just like a giant.

Lifts me on the shoulders and instant triumph.

In his arms, I know I would be safe,

No fears, no tears. What a happy place!

I dream of us walking, strolling hand in hand.

teaching me how to dance to the music from the band.

Walking me down the aisle to say I do,

just like the fairy tales and the movies too.

When I'm in pain, I run to him,

my confidant, best friend and kin.

He builds me up never lets me down.

He's always present.

What a gift from heaven!

But by morning when I awakened,

I realized in my dream I was mistaken.

The visit with my friends made me so happy.

That I dreamt my friend's dad was my daddy.

Disappointed it was a mere dream.

But in that moment, with joy, I did beam.

Now, I feel odd I have never met him, but I have no guilt,

although I wished, that special bond we could have built.

Maybe no fault of his own.

But I can never disown

that spot that should be filled with happiness,

is not present; it's void, pure emptiness.

That strong person I know is my mother.

She gives me shelter and that broad shoulder.

I cry and try; she soothes and proves

that there's no other like my mama.

She comforts and she cheers,

my only protector through the years.

I must always love her, and cherish her.

She's mother, father, sister, brother.

Filling holes and supporting roles,

building my confidence and setting goals,

bridging gaps, making sure there are no mishaps.

Yes Dad, she takes your space.

But I hope, and wonder, and wait

that someday, before it's too late,

you may show up and take your place.

So, with arms wide open, and with bated breath,

I await your appearance, will take it step by step,

to build a friendship of love and depth.

But in the meantime, of love, I'm not deprived

because my mama is standing right by my side.

4

Facing Life, Without Him

Malique's dad was an extraordinary soul who spent but a brief moment in his life and on this planet, but it was a powerful moment; it was a purposeful, meaningful and a well lived moment. His brief time here was the best years of Malique's life because they shared an unbreakable bond and a relationship of love, trust, and friendship. He missed him dearly, but his dad has left him with a rich experience that propelled him for nothing short of excellence.

He was here with us only yesterday.

But something happened; I can't relay,

that took him from me very suddenly.

And his absence could affect my destiny.

Now, my dad is nowhere to be seen, gone forever.

And I'm lost, coming to grips with seeing him, never.

That strong soldier who doted on his children,

a legacy he left so we won't be burdened.

Dad took me here, there, and everywhere.

What he has taught me, I've stored somewhere.

I modeled him; we talked about the future.

All of life's lessons I pray I have captured.

We dreamed about my path and success.

Everything I did, I knew he was impressed.

He couldn't wait to see the man I will become.

The plans I carved out, I knew he'd welcomed.

I loved to see the smile on his face when he woke me up each
morning.

I loved to say the prayers he made me repeat at sunrise and at
evening.

I missed trying to make more baskets than him on our backyard
rim,

although, I'm sure he missed them on purpose so that I can win.

But who do I look to now, and how do I plan,

to face the rest of my life without my best man?

Who would tuck me in and teach me my prayers?

Who would I share my burdens with to relieve my fears?

Whose face would I see in the audience when I pick up my awards?

And who would say "I'm so proud of you" and give me my rewards?

Who would see to it that I be the best that I can?

Who would take the job to teach me to be a man?

All I have are my memories, many, many I cherish,

filled with lessons I can draw on; I pray they never perish.

If he had some faults and flaws, they were not known.

Because only goodness and love were always shown.

Glaring in my mind's eye is the perfection in that one man,

who showed me how to speak up for myself and take a stand.

He was a role model, lived only by what he taught.

What you saw was what you got, no sham, no fraud.

He drew references of his life from his ancestors.

He taught me our history, more knowledge than professors.

He ensured that I made the right connection

to understand my decision will impact my direction.

Now I long for the day when I too, can call someone son

and tell him of the man whose love I know he would have won.

It's the reason why I smile when I wake up now.

I had a perfect model who showed me how.

5

When Cuteness Fades

Marvin was walking leisurely to the grocery store one day. An older white lady was walking in his direction about one hundred feet away. The moment she held up her head and noticed him moving toward her, she clutched her purse and raced to the other side of the street. Marvin felt hurt and stood there in wonder, wanting to cry. A feeling of disappointment engulfed him. He vowed to help erase the stereotypes society has placed on young black men and bring awareness to those who don't know them.

This is my reality, a personal story of a young black man,

of how I was adored when I was young.

As I grew older, it was a different song.

Now I'm misjudged and hardly trusted.

It seems like the goal is to get me busted.

Opinions formed; generalizations made

God forbid, with me, no chance to make a mistake.

The damage is done, but a plea for my case I make:

When mom took me out in public, their attention I gained.

They stared at me and the compliments poured like rain.

They asked me my name, and my age; they told me I'm cute, and
my big smile popped.

Then over time they noticed me less, and then the wonderful
compliments stopped.

I wondered what happened; nothing really changed, but out of
nowhere well wishes dropped.

They no longer make eye contact; they no longer look in my face.

I look at them; I examine myself; we visit the same places.

Same women, same young man, so why the grim faces?

A cause for the change I couldn't see.

Then one day it all occurred to me.

It's no puzzle. I'm growing up; that's the key.

No longer a cute baby but a young man to be.

A threat they see now, falling for the stereotype

that young black boys are budding criminals.

Their attention to me now is merely minimal.

Any simple encounter, they clutch their purses.

With fear in their eyes, they walk on the other side,

even if it is just two of us in the aisle.

What did I do between those years,

to cause this much resentment and fear?

What should I do to erase the frightening image,

they tagged on me that is causing so much damage?

How do I learn to rise above all the fret?

How do I reach them to let them know I am no threat?

Lord, open their eyes that they may see

the wonderful men, boys like me, grow up to be.

It's a challenge to be judged by the content of my character,

because my race and skin color still remain a giant factor.

But only love can fix all the worry and end all the fear.

Teaching tolerance, sensitivity, acceptance and color blindness

will end the suspicion and fear, so I can be shown pure kindness.

I will continue to walk in humility, and be sublime.

I will live my best life, placing my trust in the Divine.

I will show them love despite their hate.

Things will turn around; people will be forced to change their ways.

I am trusting God to impact them before the end of my days.

So, tolerance, love, and a positive attitude

can propel black boys to their highest altitude.

6

This Skin on Me

Zitah often enjoys the conversations with her parents about beauty and skin color. She is extremely smooth but has a very dark skin tone. She stands out in a crowd but in a beautiful way. Her friends acknowledge her beauty but oftentimes compare their light complexion to her dark skin with a hidden intent to ridicule her. Although Zitah feels sometimes disheartened that her friends try to put her down, she is not too hurt by their words because her mom taught her from the beginning to stand proud.

The color of this skin had caused me to wonder:

"Why am I so dark?" was the question I pondered.

Dad took the time to make sure I got good counsel.

Then I settled in my spirit that I won't be troubled.

When he said he doesn't want me ever to be scolded,

I knew that I had no choice but to be bold.

That's why this confidence I have must be shown:

I, am the carbon copy of my father,

the shade of his esteemed ancestors.

A purplish dark shine, with a smoothness and glow,

but a unique beauty and complexion that I'm proud to show.

From the time I can remember, Dad taught me to love my color.

"Your skin," he said, "is very dark; don't worry.

You will stand out, but stand proud; never be sorry.

As you grow older, you will understand.

That for yourself you have to stand.

They may try to taunt you, but be brave.

That should charge you; don't be afraid.

When you enter a room, people will stare at you.

Stand proud, your color is power. Don't let them faze you.

You are a princess, a unique gem; your blackness is beautiful.

Don't accept otherwise; and of that fact, be always mindful."

Now filled with confidence, I won't be deceived.

No matter what people say, I must believe:

My dark skin is the strength of my ancestors,

the love of my protectors,

the gift of the Spirit that lives in me,

and the power that God enables me.

All of this will determine what I will be.

One of the greatest success models

to boys and girls with the same struggles.

Showing the world that beauty comes in different shades and colors.

I'll open closed minds and make blind eyes see

that my dark skin color is the love, power, and beauty that surround

me.

7

This Hair on Me

Marla's hair is not as curly as Sue's nor as straight as Ben's. Her hair has a course texture, but it is not a bother to her because her mama takes great care in making her hair beautiful. But that does not mean she's not reminded by her peers that her hair texture is different. Thankfully, her mama taught her how to love herself, beginning with her hair.

My hair is special and unique,

but it took me a while to believe.

That kinky, sometimes course bundle

was once tricky to clear and untangle.

But oh, what a joy now to handle.

And when I'm clueless because I think it's a mess,

a sprinkle of my favorite mix, and it'll be at its best.

So proud of the naturalness.

Because of its texture, styles are limitless:

Cornrow, box braid, pin up, or pony tail,

I can wear afro or twist out, no style fails.

My hair is flexible, oh so versatile.

I can wear just about any hair style.

I like when I walk in the school's aisles.

And everyone commends my pretty hairstyles.

It can be kinky, curly, or straight,

different styles to create, no debate.

It fits on my head like a crown.

And when I flash my smile and look in the mirror,

a queen I see as beautiful as no other.

Mama lauds its beauty all the time.

The styles she designs, we enjoy.

God knows my hair is my pride and my joy.

No harsh chemicals to destroy its natural beauty.

It is my treasure, on show for the world to see.

Once upon a time Mom shunned its naturalness,

and used a strange substance

that destroyed the curl pattern.

Now she treats it with pure love and appreciation.

But my hair styles at times upset the big corporations,

who want me to have the style and texture like other generations.

Something about my braids, they want to ban.

When I wear it, it is somewhat problematic.

In school sometimes they won't allow it.

At work, they deem it unfit.

It's pure degradation from their lips.

But I won't be hindered by what comes from their mouths.

It's my go to hairdo; so, they better work it out.

That's the black girl style I refuse to hide.

I will continue to wear it with much love and pride

8

Say No

Drugs, in all its forms, continue to threaten our community and endanger the lives of young people. Enough attention is not given to it. Illegal drugs get into countries through cracks and crevices, and it's difficult to control. Drugs won't be a problem if the dealers have no customers. Therefore, the message that drugs destroy lives should be cemented early in the minds of our children so this horrible plague can be eradicated from our communities.

I knew the young boy, Sam, who lived next door.

I used to watch him do his exercises on the floor.

I peered at him from my bedroom window,

doing his chores and reading his kindle.

He seemed very grounded and also very smart.

His parents had given him a very good start.

He excelled in his studies; was on his way to fame.

Then one day I took a good look at his frame.

He didn't seem to look the same.

Skinny, eyes bulging, he lowered his head in shame.

He was once vibrant and very strong.

Now, something was definitely wrong.

He gazed in space and didn't seem to be fazed.

And his new behavior caused me to be amazed.

He cursed at people; then walked as if in a daze.

I asked my mom why Sam behaved like a thug.

She told me that Sam was tampering with drugs.

His parents had warned him that in drugs he shouldn't be caught.

That those temptations must definitely be fought.

But he submitted to friends, so the consequences they brought.

Now he's like a walking zombie, hanging around the public pool.

He cut his classes every day, and then dropped out of school.

His parents checked him in a rehab home.

He spent six weeks to get his habit combed.

Two weeks later, he was back on the streets

stealing things and not going home for weeks.

Then his dad searched for him again amidst all the pain.

 Sought the help Sam needed, but his efforts were in vain.

A slave Sam became to the substance.

And took it all day, in abundance.

He was found on the concrete, comatose.

He lost the battle through an overdose.

Now the family is left very heart broken.

That once promising young life was suddenly taken.

The high that drugs provide is for a moment.

When it wears off, you're left shaken and broken.

Just look and examine where drugs lead.

Then decide if that is what you really need.

They tell you just to try it once, but all it takes is that one trial

to start you up, and then you are hooked on that small vial.

Whether cannabis, inhalants, cocaine or prescription pills,

put the stop sign on your heart's door; drugs will cause you ill.

You must learn to exercise your self-will.

Try not to be the next one to cave.

Addictions are really hard to break.

It's best not to start; be really afraid.

The signs are up. Stop and beware.

I just want everyone to be aware.

Drugs can take you to an early grave.

Stand firm, SAY NO and just be brave.

9

Our Little Black Kings

Marlon is home on spring break. He has been following the news and is not happy with what he is reading and seeing. Too many bad incidences are occurring with our young black men, and he is fearful. He is concerned about his life and his future. But he is encouraged by his dad's daily reminders that injustice doesn't last forever and that a better day is coming:

When the black boy was created,

he was revered and not berated.

Was anointed king from the beginning.

He was special; everything was unlimited.

Wisdom and power were in his hands.

Wealth in abundance, great riches and land.

But he was transported to unknown plains.

And his power was suddenly contained.

Where he landed, he made his home.

Was mistreated but his story is well known.

Now this message is to all the future kings to the throne:

Your future seems challenged even as you start living.

An equal standing may not always be forthcoming.

Because of your color, others may think they're superior.

You're different, created with flavor, but never inferior.

But you are sometimes not seen for who you are.

Instead you're cast away, ignored and marred.

Singled out, left with no defense.

Can't drive, can't jog, can't walk without a problem.

Harassed, abused, accused, the issue is very solemn.

One Creator, same blood, same flesh.

But your color divides; you sometimes can't mesh.

Fences put up.

Barriers construct.

Future in jeopardy

even though you're in school to study.

Pulled over sometimes without a cause.

In the stores, followed by the security guard.

If you're not careful of the area

you'll be taken down just for pleasure.

Don't talk about your natural style of dreads

They'll harass you to take them off your head.

At the firm you may not make partner.

It's ok, your own practice you will rather.

You may be turned down on your first try.

Dust off, get up; remember you will rise.

You could be judged, abused, and condemned.

Even if you're innocent, you may receive no recompense.

The God that lives in me, I beg, please protect and amend.

So, stand tall my kings and demand equality.

Show that you can maintain your dignity.

Shoot for the stars and excel in spite of the troubles.

Show that you are capable and can work on the double.

No limit to your talent; your ideas you can match with others.

Even if the struggles are fierce, find your anchor.

And show the world that you can conquer.

Many great examples you can follow:

Malcolm, King, Mandela, Obama

Some fought, sacrificed their freedom, gave their lives for the struggle.

Keep pressing, don't give up. One day soon, we can stop the trouble.

The world would see that skin comes in different color.

And that should not diminish your worth and power.

Diversity is beautiful. Like flowers, it's a stunning arrangement,

a mix, a blend that pollinates and creates that perfect complement.

And no matter where we live and work, we will build bridges

to connect, blend, unite, and to sort out all our differences.

10

In Prison, But Unchained

Domestic abuse is at epidemic proportions and is growing rapidly. The men who vow to love the women in their lives are the ones who make the decision to end their lovers' lives. The real victims though, are the children who are left to face life without their parents and to cope with the scars that they must live with for the rest of their lives.

This story is a difficult tale for me to tell.

Its details still ring in my head like a bell.

But the story indeed needs to be heard.

Those with similar stories must hear these words.

My family was intact two weeks ago.

What suddenly happened I do not know.

All I know is that it left us so much grief.

We're slowly recovering and still in disbelief.

What I know is that my dad caused us much pain.

Something, it seems, went wrong with his brain.

He was taken in handcuffs, feet bound in shackles.

Now that image in my head, with it I must grabble.

His reason for going off to prison is still hard for me to discuss.

But the thought of what he has done leaves me with pure disgust.

Although I tried to forget what happened,

the whole ordeal left my spirit dampened.

Peaceful home, for the most part, it was filled with joy and laughter.

They tried to create a safe environment for us, their son and
daughter.

Something must have snapped.

That day everything just flapped.

No explanation still for what he did.

All I know is that we are hurting still.

It's a challenge each night even to go to my bed.

Mixed emotions are constantly flowing in my head:

I feel cheated because I can no longer nor do I want to share time
with him.

I'm missing my mother's touch, her kind deeds, and her deep love within.

I feel defeated, unable to control the shame and loss; the future
seems grim.

Confused, that he is still here,

but my mom is 6ft under there.

Livid, that I'm denied a well-rounded family life.

Fuming, when I had to seek a therapist to help with the damage.

Annoyed, when folks say to me "move on; it's time you manage."

I look at other families playing with one another.

I'm angry because I was robbed of father and mother.

Thank God for the positive people in my life

who picked up the ropes to give me that drive.

Godfathers, uncles and family have picked up the mantle

so, life's challenges I can embrace and try my best to handle.

It hasn't been easy; I miss my mother so much.

But it's hard to love dad; maybe I can, but there's no rush.

Yes, he is still my father, but I'm numb; I have no feeling.

Lord, plant forgiveness in me so I can prepare for healing.

Now I have to seek therapy,

so that I can reclaim my happy.

I must live with the mental and emotional scars.

The indelible marks are etched deep in my heart.

God knows I need full healing,

so I can live my life with meaning.

Some have said that his bad deeds his kids will inherit.

I'm here as proof that's not true; that idea has no merit.

I am NOT my father.

I walk NOT in my father's image.

My life, with God in it, I manage.

A failure I am determined not to be.

I have chosen a path, clear for all to see.

History, with me, will not repeat itself.

I am making responsible decision to emancipate myself.

I will take up the cause to rescue and revere battered women,

provide safe homes and let peace and security in it be woven.

I must work to end abuse and reverse the woman's deepest fear.

And as I seek to heal, and my hurt feelings repair,

I vow to speak out, to end all the pain and despair.

11

I'm Not Where I Live

Living in public housing is challenging. Many want to improve the quality of life for their families, but obstacles and hardships, at times, derail people's ability to reach their goals. However, with determination and hard work, big dreams can turn into reality.

Living in the home with mother and father,

poor condition but that's all they had to offer.

In the belly of the project is where we call home.

The ghettos, the slums, it is otherwise known.

We live our best lives, even with all the obstacles.

Everything in the book, you name it, upon it I stumbled:

Boy at my door, trying to get me to do his chores,

and bothering the little children to join his force.

Explosions all around me, I'm ducking from the strays.

Dice games in the walkway as I go my merry way.

Money on the table, noise to the highest levels.

Little scrabbles here and there, but then they revel.

Then sometimes they fight, harming one another.

and leave heartache, taking away each other's power.

Teen girl pregnant, unsure of the father,

left alone to fend and to be the best mother.

Strong herbs fragrant the building.

You hold your breath until you run in.

Addicts borrowing money from door to door.

You give them a dollar but they come for more.

Some parents are calling their children in, not wanting their attraction

on things that cause confusion, so they create their own distractions.

Doom looms.

How can I escape?

How do I make my way out? I silently wonder.

But Mother gripped firmly on my hand as I ponder,

telling me to, "Look straight ahead; don't pay them any mind.

Your journey is different; you have guts; you're one of a kind.

You'll walk through those doors and head off to college.

Don't come back here; just go seek some knowledge.

And when you return for a visit, it will be to inspire

those who have the ambition but lack what it requires.

The tough conditions you see now should be your drive

to work hard in school to prepare you to live a fulfilling life."

Now I move forward, with my confidence boost

believing I can achieve in whatever path I choose.

12

Forced to Entertain an Uninvited Guest

The Covid-19, Coronavirus was confirmed to have entered our shores sometime in January of 2020. After infecting millions and killing thousands, there is still no relief from this killer virus. It is a pandemic, impacting the lives of people, especially those with preexisting conditions. Its greatest impact, however, is felt in the African American community. Vaccines are in the works, but many more will die before the vaccinations take effect. The world longs for relief from this devastating invader.

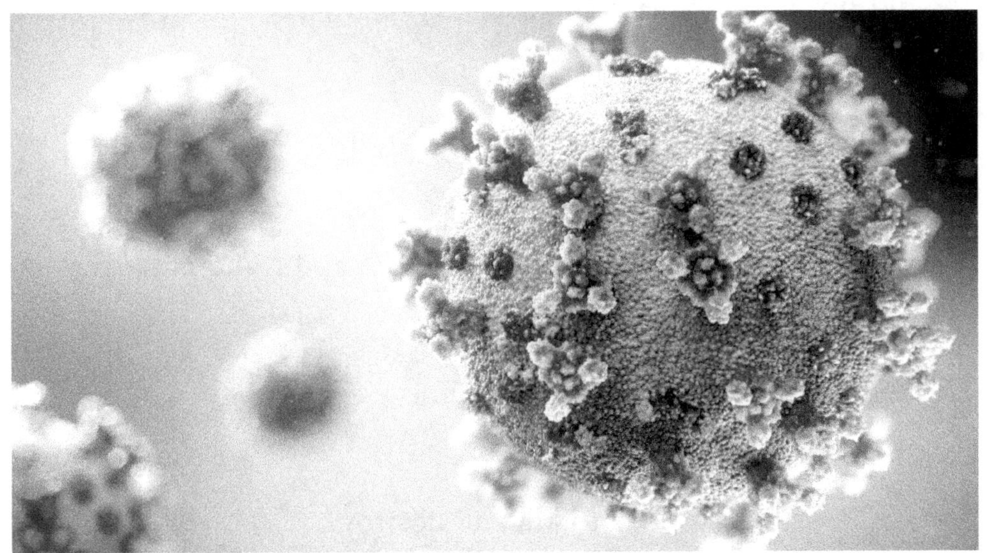

Mom always said that we must be kind to strangers; they can be angels.

Dad, on the other hand, believed that entertaining strangers can sometimes be fatal.

Maybe we should have followed Dad's advice on the dangers of strangers.

This stranger traveled miles across the globe, unprotected.

She sat next to others on airplanes, came off, and went around, uninhibited.

Legend has it that she is not of American descent.

No respecter of person's race, color, belief or accent.

It was right after my brother's wedding when she came knocking on our door.

We did not invite her in; she sneaked in anyway and destroyed us
   to the core.

We didn't know her, but she mingled, got comfortable, and then
   she never left.

She plagued and infected everyone; peace and tranquility were no
   longer kept.

She acted differently; behavior extreme.

Nothing like we have ever seen.

She came with a purpose to kill and destroy

those who ignored the rules that were employed.

So powerful, she left some with fevers; some had chills.

Some became fatigued, and all of us were desperately ill.

Others lost their smell; some lost their taste.

All sought the doctor, with no time to waste.

Some fought off pneumonia.

Some were placed on ventilators.

It was a tough fight to remain alive.

Healthcare workers toiled hard to save our lives.

It is day 30 since she entered our home.

A powerful force but not one to clone.

She has recently departed.

But left us broken hearted.

She closed schools. She shut down businesses.

Left so many testimonies and living witnesses.

She overran our hospitals, rendered some helpless.

Medical staff tried everything but was sometimes clueless.

Homes were turned into schools.

Some students struggled; they lacked the tools.

She barred people from seeing their friends.

She caused folks to wear a mask anywhere they went.

Most people work at home, distancing from the boss.

A room and zoom now accommodate the staff.

When we went out, we were careful not to mingle nor go out and about.

We tried our best to keep the monster out.

Hand sanitizers and disinfectant sprays are now a part of daily routines.

I pray they find a cure and approve all efforts to create vaccines.

We scrubbed the produce and sprayed the groceries. We washed our hands and wiped the doors.

She turned the whole world upside down. She skipped no continent and entered every shore.

And even after she destroyed so many, she turned around a second time and still came back for more.

When she invaded and pushed her way through, she stood firm with strength and power, appearing invincible.

People fought her successfully, but evidence of her presence still

lingered, so forgetting her seemed impossible.

Experts believe her eradication is possible.

But we must follow safety rules that are proven to be effective,

since black and brown people are so easily affected.

We have to take precautions and protect the vulnerable.

Apply all safety measures and do all that's applicable.

We have no immediate pharmaceutical cure.

Just some good old practices to keep us safe and sure.

Thank God, a preventative measure is finally on its way.

And if 70-80% of us take it, it would be hard for her to stay.

Ms. Covid-19, Coronavirus, stranger to our shore, enough of your

dismay.

We ask you kindly, don't enter our doors; please, leave and simply

stay away.

13

The Man I Want to Be

Addys wants to be a rocket scientist one day. He wants to go into space and explore its realm. He voices his aspirations all the time, but he is not taken seriously. His ambitions seem fanciful and to some a stretch. But he has learned to believe in himself and his abilities. If nothing else, that will see him through. There is no such theory as dreaming too big. So, for him, let the dreaming begin:

I can do anything, be anything I want to be.

Entrepreneurship is not out of reach.

I am determined that I can succeed.

In school financial literacy classes my peers never had,

but 'twill be my job to teach my brothers; they need it really bad.

Money markets, stock markets investments, you name it.

Just teach me, I'll learn; there's no limit, I can achieve it.

Tall, big and strong, they see the athlete in me.

Baseball, football, basketball, any star I can be.

But I am more than sports. My brain is made for the physicist in
me,

to find solutions and make inventions, and create my own theories
in science.

If I am the only one of my race in my class, I cannot trivialize my
presence.

This dot will be the best dot, a big dot, a special dot,

showing that I can match wisdom and ability and be what others
are not.

No group or gang necessary; they can't validate so I won't affiliate.

I'll rely on my instinct and let my own conscience be my guide.

No substance I need to alter my perception.

My high is natural so I can follow my life's direction.

14

The Woman I Will Become

Some of our young ladies lack the boldness and confidence that should have been reinforced in their homes, schools, churches and communities. Some have known nothing but ridicule and are sometimes powerless to change their direction. They lack the courage to dream big. People are quick to point out their flaws rather than their abilities. They must be encouraged to believe in themselves, find their voices, be able to chart their own course, and constantly be reminded that "You got this!"

I am encouraged to be anything I desire to be.

I will believe in my beauty, even if no one sees it but me.

My big lips, my wide nose, my dark skin, my kinky hair

are my strong attributes, at times too blind to see how beautiful

they make me.

Tall, slender and graceful, I'm pushed to be the runway model.

But that's not enough for me. I protest, and folks seem puzzled.

Same one who advised me to be all I can be

is telling me what she thinks I should or shouldn't be.

I won't settle. I want more. I have so much more potential.

I can't be detracted. I am determined to get my credentials.

Mom's words keep ringing in my ears:

"Your success should have no boundary, no limit.

Dream it, believe it, work hard, and then commit.

Jump over the hurdles and remove obstacles.

Take a detour if you must and create a spectacle."

I intend to find my purpose and ignore the noise.

I will stomp restrictions and racism, and ensure inequality, and
   sexism go away.

Then confidence, strong will, positivity, and encouragement will be
   invited to stay.

So, limitations I reject. And challenges I accept.

The astronaut, the scientist the brain surgeon, I insist.

So, if I'm told I don't have what it takes to go the distance,

I'll prove them wrong and fight hard to make my stance.

Praying for the Michelle Obama spirit within

to remove hurdles, ignore bad advice, and win.

15

A Better Day is Coming

Perfection is hard, and it seems impossible to achieve. But people can dream that one day there will be a perfect world, void of the troubles, racism, inequality, and other problems. They have that glimmer of hope that someday, in the not-too-distant future, things will get better because injustices will not reign forever:

I dream of a city without walls.

No poor, no rich, justice for all.

The people of color whose experiences were usually solemn

can now live anywhere and move freely without a problem.

I dream of a school where everyone: black, white, or brown is
    accepted.

No affirmative action, no wait list, a place where no one is rejected.

I see boy, I see girl of other race, culture and different color,

living like brother and sister, in homes with father and mother.

I see uniform houses, different designs, but equal value,

living in peace, and harmony with clearly written statutes.

No need for gate, no need for guard.

Everyone is seen working very hard.

The leadership is astute and his judgment is fair.

No malice, no hate, anything amiss is easily repaired.

No stealing, no need to, because everything is in abundance.

No pain, no heartache; only love takes dominance.

No violence, no crime; everyone is in one accord.

Kindness is given, gratitude received, not a bad deed to record.

Where will you find that? The outsiders want to doubt.

But I rebuke the negative words from their mouths.

Not everyone could be a member.

No room for skeptics, please remember.

You must believe that some place, somewhere there's a utopia.

For those who no longer want to be a part of society's dystopia.

Bio

Mrs. Nurseen Davis was born on the island of St. Vincent and the Grenadines, where she lived for the first eighteen years of her life. She migrated to United States, Virgin Islands where she attended college and graduate school. She taught English at the junior high school and high school levels for over 28 years. She also taught reading to non-matriculated students at the college level. Nurseen served as the Language Arts Coordinator of the St. Thomas-St. John district before she retired in 2016. She has two adult children, Cozette and Cosville Rogers, and she resides in Hendersonville, North Carolina and St. Thomas, Virgin Islands with her husband, Charles Davis. She took up her second love, writing, post retirement and has published Brighten the Corner Stories: Children's Challenges and Triumphs. Brighten the Corner Stories Too: Affirmations for Children of Color is her second book.

www.ingramcontent.com/pod-product-compliance
Lightning Source LLC
Chambersburg PA
CBHW060601100726
47907CB00005B/1462